5 Minute Holiday Classics

5 Minute Holiday Classics

FOR
YOUNG
READERS

First published in various editions from c. 1890–1923.

First Racehorse for Young Readers Edition 2019.

All rights to any and all materials in copyright owned by the publisher are strictly reserved by the publisher.

Racehorse for Young Readers books may be purchased in bulk at special discounts for sales promotion, corporate gifts, fund-raising, or educational purposes. Special editions can also be created to specifications. For details, contact the Special Sales Department, Racehorse for Young Readers, 307 West 36th Street, 11th Floor, New York, NY 10018 or info@skyhorsepublishing.com.

Racehorse for Young Readers ™ is a pending trademark of Skyhorse Publishing, Inc.®, a Delaware corporation.

Visit our website at www.skyhorsepublishing.com.

10 9 8 7 6 5 4 3 2 1

Library of Congress Cataloging-in-Publication Data is available on file.

Book design by Daniel Brount

Print ISBN: 978-1-63158-340-7
Ebook ISBN: 978-1-63158-342-1

Printed in China

Contents

Around the World with Santa Claus

BY Santa Claus two little folks,
wee Fred and sister Flo,
Have been invited on a trip
around the world to go;

A trip on which they'll have a chance
not often given to see

All countries they have read about in
their Geography.

You see them here about to start in
Santa's famous sleigh;

His reindeer team is ready to bear
them swift away;

And with them they are taking an
abundant stock of toys

To fill the Christmas stockings of
delighted girls and boys.

Though we may travel well enough
On dry land with a team,
When we wish to cross the ocean
We have to take to steam.
Old Santa much enjoys the trip,
And says there's nothing finer
Than to sniff the breeze upon the deck
Of a crack Atlantic "Liner."

The voyage o'er without mishap,
We land on Britain's Isle,
And take a cab, on top of which
Our trunks and traps we pile;
The jolly streetboys Santa spy,
And give him lots of chaff,
But at that game he's quite their
    match,
And on them turns the laugh.

For those who love good feeding, here's a sight that's very jolly
   Plum-pudding most delicious, and Boar's-head decked with holly;
Of old in Merrie England, they were borne on Christmas Day,
   Unto the castle table in this stately, pompous way.
The guests, no doubt, delayed not to clear them from the plate,
   For good things tasted then as well as at the present date.

In the frosty land of Norway, folks fasten to their feet
Long wooden skates called skis, with which they travel very fleet;
So Santa and his party put on a pair of these,
And down the icy hill-sides dart through the wintry breeze.

To the ever frozen regions of the Northern Frigid Zone,
To the home of the seal and walrus and the Eskimo we've flown:
But though this chilly atmosphere may suit the polar bear,
We think that for our own part we prefer a milder air,
So not very much extended will be our visit here,
And we soon shall take departure for a climate not so drear.

A scene this is in Germany:
Upon the left appears

Rupert, a grim fiend whom
every youngster fears,

Beside him is the Christ-child,
arrayed in garments white,

While St. Peter, with his keys in
hand, stands forth upon the right,

In the centre is St. Nicholas, the
Bishop kind and good,

Who's the friend of all young
people who behave just as they
should.

To every house the party comes
on Christmas Eve to hear

How all the little boys and girls
have acted through the year;

For those who've not been
naughty, nor parents caused to
grieve,

Upon the lighted Christmas-
tree they pretty presents leave,

But those of whose behavior
they get a bad report,

Receive a gift from, Rupert, not
of a pleasant sort.

On Christmas Eve in Holland, through the queer old peak-roofed towns
St. Nicholas the kind-hearted on a donkey goes his rounds,
With nice presents in his basket for each obedient child,
And nothing for the naughty ones who have been bad and wild.
A new brother or new sister, the children there are taught,
By the stork, a funny long-legged bird, has to the house been brought,
And of course it always causes a more intense delight,
If his Storkship brings the stranger as a gift on Christmas night.

GLORIA · IN · EXCELSIS ·

The Bambino

This tableau forms in Italy's clime
A favorite pageant at Christmas-time
The crib is shown of the Holy Child,
With his mother, Mary, and Joseph mild;

Shepherds adore, and Angels above
Chant their message of peace and love,
While Bethlehem's Star sends down its ray
To guide the Wise Men on their way.

O'er the lonely, sterile wastes of Arabia's desert land,
No beasts except the camels can travel through the sand;
So Santa Claus upon their backs bestows his precious freight,
Then climbs aloft himself and rides along in solemn state.

To have it warm at Christmas, to us seems very peculiar,
But in Australian lands that is the warmest time of year:
Santa can't get reindeer here, so the only thing to do,
Is to travel round upon the back of a bounding kangaroo.

And in the U.S.A.
Canoeing is exciting when the stream is wild and rough.
And Santa looks as if he thought he'd had about enough;
He wears, you see, an aspect of great comfort and relief,
When he seats himself to smoke a pipe with the friendly
  Indian Chief.

We are now in California, and pause to have a sight
Of the trees that are so famous for their monstrous girth and height.
As we pass in grand procession, our pets may be inspected;
A very happy family, indeed, we have collected.
They behave toward each other in a style polite and pleasing—
That is all except the parrots, who are quite too fond of teasing.

At last the journey's finished; its excitements all are o'er;

Strange sights and foreign wonders have been gazed at by the score;

The world has been inspected, North and South, and West and East,

And our travelers now celebrate their doings with a feast.

At a table spread with eatables and drinkables the best,

They are seated, with good Santa as the most exalted guest;

And as the gay proceedings are approaching to a close,

This toast young Master Frederick arises to propose:

"Here's a health to Santa Claus, the friend of girls and boys;

May his heart be ever full of mirth—his pack be full of toys!"

Father

Christmas

T HE day of all the year to me
Dawns with the Christmas
morning;
For then we bring bright
Christmas greens
The dear old home adorning.

For every heart is filled with love,
Each makes its own confession;
The garlands that we twine today
Are but love's sweet expression.

My mother does the nicest things,
When Christmas Day is here,
She fills big baskets full of stuff
To give the poor some cheer.

Oh, what jolly fun we have
At our parties gay!
Music, laughter, song and dance—
For 'tis Christmas Day!

Mistletoe and holly,
Berries white and red,
All our rooms adorning,
'Round and overhead.
How you warm the pulses,
How the heart grows light
When we weave your colors
In a garland bright!

Mistletoe and holly,
You are friends of ours,
And your waxen berries
Fairer are than flowers;
Braving winter tempests,
Smiling through the snow,
How you cheer our spirits
With your waxen glow!

Mistletoe and holly,
Smile on us today,
While in mirth and revel
Hours are passed away
Then the recollection
Of your dainty hues
Shall, with us abiding,
Bring the dreams we choose.

Hurrah! the fields are all
white with snow
But green as ever his
branches glow;
In winter or summer, no
change knows he—
He's always our dear old
Christmas tree!

Dear Grandmamma, here's something
That Santa left for you;
I hope that you will like it—
I'm sure 'tis nice and new.

The children now come
    hurrying down,
All crowding, running,
    shouting!
To see if it is really true,—
It seems to me they're
    doubting—
But soon they see Santa's
    been here
And brought us lots of
    Christmas cheer.

Put on your great-coat and
    mittens,
Bring out your Christmas
    sled,
Hear the sweet sleigh-bells
    a-jingling,
All other noises have fled.
Now let your glad voices
    ring,
For winter is king!

Come one, come all, come
    great and small,
This is the pleasure that
    never grows tame,
At morning and evening,
    and every hour,
And year after year it is
    ever the same.
Hurrah! hurrah! may it
    ever be so,
Then we shall never grow
    old, you know.

Over the ice, so
    smooth and bright,
How we skim along!
This is one of the
    merriest sports
Which to girls and
    boys belong.

Hurrah! hurrah for
    the ice and snow,
For our limbs are
    strong and fleet,
    you know.

Frosted are pavement and
    window,
Frozen are pond and
    brook,
Snowflakes have fallen by
    thousands,
We are in fairyland—look!

Men and women, children, babes,
Joyful wake—'tis Christmas Day!
Birds, sing out your sweetest songs;
Sun, shine forth your brightest ray.
Let all hearts with gladness bound,
Let all hearts be good and true;
"Peace on earth, good-will around,"
Be our motto, ever new.

And let those who
thus rejoice
Christmas carols
gladly raise,
Joining heart, and
soul, and voice
In our Christmas
hymns of praise.

Is There a Santa Claus?

Is There a Santa Claus?

A Great Editor's Answer to a Little Girl's Question

How the Little Girl Asked the Question

MANY years ago a little girl who was beginning to have her doubts about the reality of Santa Claus wrote this letter to the *New York Sun*:

Dear Editor:

I am 8 years old. Some of my little friends say there is no Santa Clause. Papa says, "If you see it in the Sun, it's so." Please tell me the truth; is there a Santa Claus?

Virginia O'Hanlon

In reply to this childish letter, Chas. A. Dana, one of the greatest American editors, wrote and published his famous answer which has become the Christmas classic of America.

How the Great Editor Stilled Virginia's Doubts

VIRGINIA, your little friends are wrong.
They have been affected by the skepticism of a skeptical age. They do not believe except they see. They think that nothing can be which is not comprehensible by their little minds. All minds, Virginia, whether they be men's or children's, are little.

In this great universe of ours man is a mere insect, an ant in his intellect, as compared with the boundless world about him, as measured by the intelligence capable of grasping the whole of truth and knowledge.

YES, Virginia, there is a Santa Claus. He exists as certainly as love and generosity and devotion exist, and you know that they abound and give to your life its highest beauty and joy.

Alas! how dreary would be the world if there were no Santa Claus! It would be as dreary as if there were no Virginias. There would be no childlike faith then, no poetry, no romance to make tolerable this existence. We should have no enjoyment, except in sense and sight. The eternal light with which childhood fills the world would be extinguished.

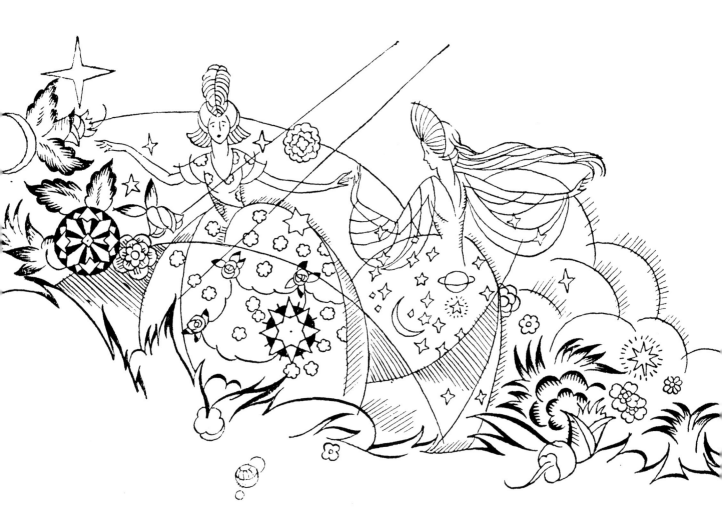

NOT believe in Santa Claus! You might as well not believe in Fairies! You might get your papa to hire men to watch in chimneys on Christmas evening to catch Santa Claus, but even if they did not see Santa Claus coming down what would that prove? Nobody sees Santa Claus, but that is no sign that there is no Santa Claus. The most real things in the world are those that neither children nor men can see.

Did you ever see Fairies dancing on the lawn? Of course not, but that's no proof that they are not there. Nobody can conceive or imagine all the wonders there are unseen and un-seeable in the world.

YOU may tear apart the baby's rattle and see what makes the noise inside, but there is a veil covering the unseen world which not the strongest man, nor even the united strength of all the strongest men that ever lived, could tear apart. Only faith, fancy, poetry, love, romance, can push aside that curtain and view and picture the supernal beauty and glory beyond.

Is it real? Ah, Virginia, in all this world there is nothing else real and abiding.

NO Santa Claus? Thank God, he lives and he lives forever. A thousand years from now, Virginia, nay ten times ten thousand years from now, he will continue to make glad the heart of childhood.

A Letter from Old Father Christmas

HERE I am once more, my dear children and people, all! and very glad I am to come, as I know you welcome me with all your hearts.

You, my young friends, never grow tired of me, and you often wish that I could come to you before the right time and make a long stay with you. My visits are short, but I try to make them as merry as possible and to bring my baskets and bags full of presents for every one, young and old, rich and poor alike.

Did you ever wonder where I live and what becomes of me all the year through from Christmas time to Christmas time? I really do not believe you ever thought of that.

Well, I live in a very wonderful place, very far away from you, but just whereabouts that place is, I shall not tell you, partly because I do not want you to come, any army of restless little children, to rouse me up and to ask to come soon to your homes, and partly because if I told you where I live you would know too much.

All I shall say is that it is in the far North and that I sleep a great deal through the summer time and on Midsummer's Day I do not wake at all.

Then, when the year is growing old, I shake myself and gather up my wits again, and begin to make all sorts of presents for people, pack my baggage, and then I walk off, carrying my heavy loads. I travel with the sun, from East to West, so I arrive in all the countries one after another.

At last I come back to my own home, where I rest after my rapid journey round the world. Many lands do I see, many are the homes I visit, many are the trees I find waiting to be hung all over with presents, and many are the stockings hanging on children's beds for me to fill—while the dear little heads are fast asleep on the pillows, although these same little heads had said that they would not go to sleep until they saw Father Christmas or Santa Claus or whatever they like to call me, coming to put things into their stockings.

So, having said all this, I must now wish
you good-day, good-night, and good-cheer,
and always remain your loving *old Father
Christmas*.

The
Snow-Man

THE pretty white snow-flakes had been falling, falling for two days or more, and now they had ceased, and lay all over the ground like a soft blanket. The sun shone brightly once more, and Nettie begged for leave to go out and help her brothers to build up a great snow-man, whose progress she had been watching from the school-room window. So out into the garden she went, well wrapped up and with her thick boots on, and she grew very warm and rosy digging in the snow with her little wooden spade. "Oh Mother, it is great fun," she cried out. "Do let me stay until the snow-man is finished. He is to be called Father Christmas, and he will have a crown of ivy on his head and stones for his eyes, and oh, how nice it is to make Father Christmas, for this is Christmas time."

At last the man of snow was finished, and when the children had gone into the house they remained gazing at him from the windows. They had worked hard to build him up nicely and he was indeed, they thought, a fine figure. To complete his head and to put on a wreath of ivy, they had borrowed a stepladder from the gardener, and they had placed a long stick in his hand.

Tea hour came, and the blinds had to be drawn down. "Tomorrow will be Christmas day," said Willie. "We shall make him larger and taller and grander than he is now."

Two or three hours later, when the children were going to bed, they peeped out through the windows and saw that the moon had risen, and was shining on their old snow-man, and making him look larger and more solemn than in the daylight. His shadow lay long and dark behind him on the grass. Nettie thought it was a wonderful thing to look at, and she ran and fetched her mother to come and see it, and it was so hard for her to leave the window, that mother had at last to carry her off to bed, where her head had no sooner been comfortably placed on the pillow, and her bright eyes had closed, than she fell into a sound sleep and found herself in the land of dreams. A very curious and beautiful land it was, where old Father Christmas was king.

He took little Nettie by the hand, and led her about among hills all covered with snow, on which the sun shone brightly, and where she saw tall white lilies growing, but it did not occur to her that she had never seen white lilies growing in snow before. The sun, the moon and the stars were all shining brightly together up in the blue sky, but that did not matter, for everything seemed quite natural there.

At last old Father Christmas led her to a large house, where she saw a table covered all over with beautiful Christmas presents, some for herself; then he sat down and told her to fetch her brothers, and to carry away all their presents, and she, in state of wild delight was just going to jump up and to throw her arms round his neck, when she suddenly awoke, and saw Nurse drawing up the nursery blinds.

"Come, Miss Nettie," said she, "get up and see if Father Christmas has put anything into your stocking."

"Oh, Nurse, I have just been walking with him in my dream, and I want to see if he is still out on the lawn." So out of bed jumped Nettie, ran across the floor, and, kneeling on a chair, looked out of the window down into the garden, but in vain did she try to find the snow-man;—where he had stood so proudly yesterday, there was nothing but a shapeless heap! Drip, drop, splash, gurgle, came from every roof and spout where the melted snow was running fast away, for, alas! early, early in the morning, a sudden thaw had come on, and now the snow, so thick and bright the day before, was fast disappearing, and with it the old snow-man.

Poor Nettie gazed until the tears began to gather in her eyes, but turning round to ask Nurse to look at the sad sight, she spied a very fat stocking hanging on the foot of her bed, and springing forward to take possession of it, her disappointment was soon forgotten in examining the contents—oranges, apples, raisins, nuts, bonbons, a sweet little doll, and a pinscushion like a heart, with "Nettie" printed on one side in shining pins-heads, and on the top, for a little joke, was a small lump of coal wrapped up in paper!

Nettie jumped for joy, while shouts and laughter from the boys room told of delightful stockings for them too. But now it was almost breakfast time and they must get dressed as quickly as possible and run down to kiss father and mother, and give them some little Christmas presents which had, with Nurse's kind help, been made ready with wonderful secrecy. But here fresh surprises awaited the children, for beside their plates lay lovely toys and gifts for each, too many to describe now. So good old Father Christmas had not forgotten the children, and Nettie's dream came true after all!

Merry
Christmas
ABC

A B C D

E F G H

I J K L

M N O P

Q R S T

U V W X

Y Z

A is for **APPLE** that hangs on the tree.

B is for **BELLS** that chime out in glee.

C is for **CANDY** to please boys and girls.

D is for **DOLLY** with long flaxen curls.

E is for **EVERGREENS** decking the room.

F is for **FLOWERS** of sweetest perfume.

G is for **GIFTS** that bring us delight,

H is for **HOLLY** with red berries bright.

I is for **ICE**, so shining and clear.

J is the **JINGLE** of bells far and near.

K is **KRISS KRINGLE** with fur cap and coat.

I WANT
A SLED A
LIVE HORS
A JACKNI
FE A
STABEL
A DRUM
PLEAS GIV
ME EVERY
THING I
CANT THINK
OF

SANTA
CLOUS

SANTA
CLOS

KRIS
KRINGL

DEAR
SANTA
CLAUS

Sandy
Claus

L is for **LETTERS** the children all wrote.

M is for MISTLETOE shining like wax.

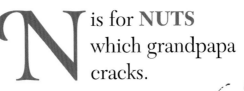

N is for **NUTS** which grandpapa cracks.

O is for ORANGES yellow and sweet.

P is **PLUM PUDDING** a holiday treat.

Q the **QUADRILLE**
in which each one
must dance.

R for the **REINDEER**
that gallop and
prance.

S is for
SNOW
that falls
silently down.

T is for **TURKEY** so
tender and brown.

U is for **UPROAR** that goes on all day.

V is for **VOICES** that carol this day.

W for **WREATHS** hung up on the wall.

X is for **X-MAS** with pleasures for all.

Y is for **YULE-LOG**
that burns clear
and bright.

Z is for **ZEST**
shown from
morning till night.

The Night Before Christmas

'TWAS the night before Christmas, when all through the house
    Not a creature was stirring, not even a mouse;
    The stockings were hung by the chimney with care,
In hopes that St. Nicholas soon would be there;

THE children were nestled all snug in their beds,
  While visions of sugar-plums danced through their heads;
And Mamma in her kerchief and I in my cap
Had just settled our brains for a long winter's nap,
When out on the lawn there arose such a clatter,

I SPRANG from my bed to see what was the matter.
Away to the window I flew like a flash,
Tore open the shutters and threw up the sash.
The moon, on the breast of the new-fallen snow,
Gave a lustre of mid-day to objects below;

WHEN what to my wandering eyes should appear
But a miniature sleigh and eight tiny reindeer,
With a little old driver, so lively and quick,
I knew in a moment it must be St. Nick.
More rapid than eagles his coursers they came,

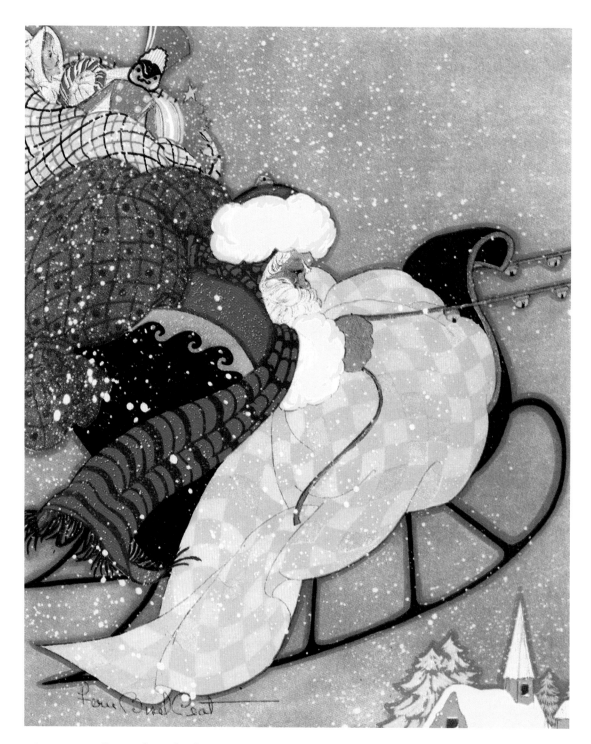

AND he whistled, and shouted, and called them by name:
"Now, Dasher! now, Dancer! now, Prancer! now, Vixen!
On, Comet! on, Cupid! on, Donder and Blitzen!—
To the top of the porch, to the top of the wall!
Now dash away, dash away, dash away all!"

A S dry leaves before the wild hurricane fly,
When they meet with an obstacle, mount to the sky,
So up to the house-top the coursers they flew,
With a sleigh full of toys, and St. Nicholas, too.

AND then in a twinkling I heard on the roof
The prancing and pawing of each little hoof.
As I drew in my head, and was turning around,
Down the chimney St. Nicholas came with a bound.
He was dressed all in fur from his head to his foot,

AND his clothes were all tarnished with ashes and soot;
A bundle of toys he had flung on his back,
And he looked like a peddler just opening his pack.
His eyes how they twinkled! his dimples how merry!
His cheeks were like roses, his nose like a cherry.

HIS droll little mouth was drawn up like a bow,
And the beard on his chin was as white as the snow.
The stump of a pipe he held tight in his teeth,
And the smoke, it encircled his head like a wreath.

H E had a broad face, and a round little belly
That shook when he laughed, like a bowl full of jelly.
He was chubby and plump—a right jolly old elf—
And I laughed when I saw him, in spite of myself.
A wink of his eye, and a twist of his head,

SOON gave me to know I had nothing to dread.
He spake not a word, but went straight to his work,
And filled all the stockings; then turned with a jerk,
And laying his finger aside of his nose,
And giving a nod, up the chimney he rose.

HE sprang to his sleigh, to his team gave a whistle,
And away they all flew like the down of a thistle;
But I heard him exclaim, ere he drove out of sight,
"Happy Christmas to all, and to all a good-night!"

The Nutcracker
of Nuremberg

GREETINGS!

WE present here the story that inspired Peter Tchaikovsky to compose his immortal *Nutcracker Suite* which had its premiere as a ballet in St. Petersburg, Russia, in 1892. It was revised a short time later into the everlastingly charming and popular Suite that we know today.

The story underlying the music has many versions and so reviewers have presented conflicting summaries. However, it seems agreed that the basis used by Tchaikovsky was *The Nutcracker of Nuremberg* by Alexander Dumas, although that, in turn, was based on *Nutcracker and Mouse-King*, an earlier story by a German, E.T. A. Hoffmann.

The specific dances of the suite are not mentioned in the tale but appear to have been Tchaikovsky's interpretations of things that might have taken place in the wonderful Kingdom of Dolls, described in the book.

Dumas's story is so full of delicate charm and embodies so completely the humor, mystery, excitement and fantasy of Christmas, that we present to you this illustrated synopsis with the hope that it may serve as your portal to that nebulous land—that wonderful, glittering, fairy-kissed land—where the children dwell at Christmas-time.

To children, one and one-hundred-and-one, we dedicate this volume, and wish them one and all the merriest kind of a Christmas.

HAPPY ADVENTURING

THE NUTCRACKER OF NUREMBERG

IT was Christmas Eve at the home of President Silberhaus, Chief Justice of the fabulous old city of Nuremberg.

In the dining room, his two children, Marie, a delicate dreamy child of seven, and Fritz, a robust, militant boy of nine, waited breathlessly at the doors of the salon, through which mysterious sounds of Christmas preparation had issued all day long. As their eyes grew round with expectancy, angelic music floated softly to their ears.

Then a bell pealed, the doors opened, and the children rushed into the wonder-filled room. But they stopped transfixed before a festooned Christmas tree that glittered with a thousand fairy candles and had strewn beneath it presents of every description.

Roused to action by their parents, the children fell to exploring their gifts. Fritz found a squadron of gorgeously attired Hussars mounted on sleek, white horses. There was a large, bridled chestnut, which he rode spiritedly around the room. Marie discovered a charming silk dress and a beautiful doll.

At that moment Godfather Drosselmayer appeared and the children ran to greet him. He was an old man of wry aspect, and the possessor of a droll and vivacious imagination. His mechanical skill, especially with toys and clocks, was so great that he was venerated almost as a wizard.

He presented the children a fanciful chateau of his own making. Its beauty and the tiny moving figures within delighted Marie. However, since it was too delicate for her and Fritz to handle, they returned to the simpler presents beneath the tree.

There, in the shelter of the lower branches, Marie discovered a charming little wooden man that she had overlooked before. Although his painted face, with its cotton beard, was much too big for his body, it wore a benevolent expression, which drew her irresistibly. He was attired as a gentleman in a real velvet suit, but his peasant cap and strange wooden cape that hung stiffly down his back puzzled her.

Noting his daughter's interest in the quaint fellow, President Silberhaus picked him up. When he raised the wooden cape, the little man's mouth opened wide enough for a nut to be inserted. When he pressed it down again, the nut cracked.

Marie was delighted with the nutcracker, but her pleasure was short-lived, for Fritz demanded his turn at using it and broke the poor little fellow's jaw.

Marie, in a burst of maternal solicitude, bandaged the wound with a piece of ribbon and held Nutcracker closely to her, defending him, even against the mischievous glances of Godfather Drosselmayer.

That night she was granted permission to remain in the salon, after Godfather had left and the family had retired, in order to put her wounded Nutcracker comfortably to bed in the big glass toy cabinet.

When the clock struck midnight, she looked, and in the dim light she fancied she saw Godfather Drosselmayer perched on its top. At the same instant, an army of mice, led by Mouse-King, wearing seven crowns on his seven heads, burst into the room. In awe, Marie backed against the cabinet door and shattered the glass with her elbow. With that, the cupboard became luminous, the toys inside sprang to life and Nutcracker leaped to the edge of his shelf, wielding a saber, defying Mouse-King and inciting the toys to combat. He snatched Marie's ribbon bandage from his wounded jaw, carried it to his lips with great feeling, tied it around his waist and jumped to the floor. All

the toys surged after him and engaged the mouse army in a terrific battle. Victory wavered uncertainly, but finally through the smoke and confusion, Marie spied Nutcracker. Mouse-King was upon him and she knew that although her hero had fought valiantly, he was in a desperate spot. She threw her slipper. It hit Mouse-King and PPF!—like magic—the toys and mice all disappeared.

Marie awakened in the morning, surprised to be in her own bed with a bandage on her elbow. She related her exciting midnight adventure to her mother, who stood peering anxiously down at her. But instead of being impressed, the good lady smiled and said that the curious experience was only a bad dream that had resulted from the cut Marie had received when she put her elbow through the toy cabinet door. But when Godfather Drosselmayer heard the tale, he nodded solemnly and disclosed in a strange story that Nutcracker was really his handsome nephew, Nathaniel Drosselmayer, who had earned the right to be a prince through an act of heroism. He said his wooden form was due to an enchantment of the mice, whom the act had displeased, and so the Mouse-King was pledged to pursue Nutcracker until his grudge should be entirely satisfied.

Godfather also foretold that Nutcracker's human form would be restored only after a charming young lady had declared her love to him and the Mouse-King had been vanquished.

In Marie's imaginative mind, Nutcracker became the enchanted young Drosselmayer.

On three successive nights, when Mouse-King exacted sweetmeats of her to ransom Nutcracker's life, she supplied them.

Then, gallantly, Nutcracker demanded a sword to replace the one he had lost in battle. On the fourth night at twelve, he tapped on Marie's bedroom door, presented her the slain Mouse-King's seven crowns and invited her to accompany him.

She followed him along the dimly lit hall to the open clothes closet. Together, they ascended a tiny staircase that led up through her father's coat sleeve.

A great light shone, and there before them glittered the Kingdom of Dolls. They walked amid houses built of marzipan and other sweetmeats, meadows of sugar candy and rivers of perfumed orangeade.

Finally they came to the Christmas Forest, a-shimmer with ten thousand lights. Nutcracker clapped his hands, and quaint little candy shepherds and

shepherdesses, hunters and huntresses came out to greet them. They presented Marie a chocolate nougat stool with a licorice cushion, and bade her be seated. Then, in a charming manner, they performed a ballet to the tune of hunting horns. Marie was delighted, but Nutcracker said they must not tarry and led her on toward the capital city.

They crossed the Essence of Roses River in a jeweled chariot and went by places that looked like Godfather Drosselmayer's toy chateau. Finally they passed through tall, glacé fruit gates between rows of silver soldiers, who presented arms and cried, "Welcome, dear Prince, to the Capital City of Jam!"

Marie was impressed by the title accorded Nutcracker, but before she could exclaim, he swept her on to the main marketplace of the city. There a joyous and noisy population, made up of dolls of every description from all corners of the world, milled about. They laughed and talked, danced and sang, and even staged parades. Some drank free orangeade that gushed from a huge sweetbun fountain, while others scooped whipped cream from communal bowls that were clustered about it.

Marie was so enthralled, she scarcely realized that Nutcracker was leading her steadily onward and upward.

"The Palace of the Marzipans!" he announced suddenly and stopped before a majestic doorway. Marie's wide eyes ran swiftly over the magnificent building that rose before her. The walls were constructed of candy flowers and mounted to aerial turrets so high that they seemed lost in filmy pink mist.

Silvery music brought Marie's attention back down to the great doors, which were slowly swinging open. As she and Nutcracker entered amid much pomp, four beautiful doll princesses fell upon the little man calling him brother and Prince. When he introduced Marie and explained to them how he cherished her because she had saved his life by throwing her slipper and by furnishing him the sword with which he had slain Mouse-King, they greeted her with affection and escorted her and Nutcracker into a beautiful room of the palace.

They started to prepare a repast of tiny cakes, candied fruits and marzipan, but Marie floated away, higher and higher until paff! she fell from an immeasurable height.

She opened astonished eyes. "Where was I? Where am I?" she stammered, and then in a voice full of awe, she related the marvelous adventure in the Kingdom of Dolls to her mother, who was leaning over her bed in the bright morning sunlight.

There was a burst of laughter. The family with Godfather Drosselmayer had been listening at the bedroom door.

Although everyone agreed that Marie had been dreaming, she insisted that everything had really happened, and to prove it, she produced seven tiny crowns, all exquisitely wrought from pure gold.

"See, here are the Mouse-King's crowns which Nutcracker, the young Mr. Drosselmayer, gave me!"

The family was impressed, but Godfather Drosselmayer recalled to them that the crowns were watch charms, that he had given to Marie on her second birthday.

"Why, Godfather!" the little girl exclaimed, "you know all about it. Confess that Nutcracker, your nephew Nathaniel, gave me the seven crowns!"

Godfather cocked his head and fastened a canny eye upon the little girl, but he said nothing.

No one believed her! Marie knew that she must henceforth keep her beautiful experiences to herself or be thought a lunatic by everyone. So, as the years passed, her silence and far-away manner won her the name of "Little Dreamer."

One day when Marie was nearing her sixteenth birthday, she sat contemplating Nutcracker in the glass toy cabinet. He was well now; his broken jaw had long since been mended and he seemed to smile, as of old, in his gently benevolent manner. Godfather Drosselmayer, who sat nearby repairing a clock, glanced now and then at Marie and chuckled amusedly.

Suddenly, oblivious of Godfather's presence, Marie proclaimed aloud to the little wooden man, "I love you!"

There was a crash. She fell from her chair in a swoon.

When she finally came to her senses, she was in the arms of her mother who was saying, "How can a big girl like you be silly enough to fall from a chair? Come get up, I have news for you. Godfather's nephew, Nathaniel Drosselmayer, who has just arrived in Nuremberg from his travels abroad, is here at our house in search of his uncle. See, here both of them come now!"

Marie smoothed her dress, patted her hair and turned to see Godfather Drosselmayer advancing and holding by the hand an extraordinarily handsome young man, who bowed and greeted Marie in a charming manner. He placed at her feet flowers and quantities of the most excellent marzipan and bon bons she had ever eaten, outside of the Kingdom of Dolls.

Later, at the dinner table after the dessert had been served, Marie watched gravely as the charming young man cracked nuts for the whole family. When he placed them between his teeth and pulled his queue, they cracked and fell apart in just the right fashion.

This accomplishment seemed to please Godfather Drosselmayer, for he chuckled merrily. In fact the whole family, and even the young man himself, all looked enormously pleased.

Marie had blushed deeply when she first saw Nathaniel, and became even more flustered when, after dinner, he suggested that they return to the salon, where the big toy cabinet stood.

Scarcely were they alone, when he fell on one knee and said, "O excellent Mademoiselle Silberhaus, you see here the happy Drosselmayer, whose life you once saved in this very room. I lost the enchanted form of the Nutcracker when you, a young and beautiful maiden, proclaimed your love. If, dear lady, you still feel the same toward me, I beg the honor of your hand, to share my throne and to reign with me over the Kingdom of the Dolls."

Marie gently raised young Drosselmayer up and said to him, "You are kind and good, Monsieur, and as you have, in addition, a wonderful kingdom full of magnificent palaces and jolly subjects, I accept your offer provided my father and mother consent."

The door of the salon had opened a little while before, quite without the knowledge of the young people, all engrossed in their own affairs, and the President, his wife, and Godfather Drosselmayer now advanced applauding.

Marie was red as a cherry with excitement but the young man, quite composed, advanced toward the President and his wife. Saluting courteously, he made them a handsome speech asking for Marie's hand. This was graciously accorded him on condition that the marriage should not take place before a year.

Time passed slowly, as you can imagine, but finally the momentous day arrived and the prince came back for his bride in a little carriage of mother-of-pearl encrusted with gold and silver. It was drawn by horses no larger than sheep and priceless in value since there were no others like them in the world. He led her to the Marzipan Palace where they were married by the house chaplain. Twenty-two thousand little people all covered with pearls, diamonds, and other precious stones danced at their wedding.

And so it was that Marie and the restored Nutcracker became the rulers of the wonderful Kingdom of Dolls. And do you know, to this very day they still reign over that beautiful kingdom, where one may see everywhere shining Christmas forests, rivers of orange juice and essence of roses, diaphanous palaces of sugar finer than snow and more transparent than ice—and, in fact, all sorts of other magnificent and miraculous things, provided one's eyes are good enough to see them.

Santa Claus
and his Works

THIS nice little story for girls and for boys,
Is all about Santa Claus, Christmas, and toys,
So listen, my children, to what you shall hear,
For I know, to each little one, Santa is dear.

In a nice little village called Santa Claus-ville,
With its houses and church, at the foot of the hill,
Lives jolly old Santa Claus—day after day,
He works and he whistles the moments away.

For he knows that in labor is happiness found,
And a merrier fellow was never around;
So, fat and good natured, this jolly old chap
Will never be idle, except for a nap.

From houses and furniture, dishes and pans,
To bracelets and brooches, and bright colored fans,
And soldiers and pop-guns, and trumpets and drums,
To baby's tin rattle, and bright top which hums.

And oh, the gay dollies with long curling hair,
That can open their eyes and sit up in a chair.
There old Santa will sit with his specs on his nose
And work all the day making pretty new clothes;

Such as dresses and sashes, and hats for the head,
And night-gowns to wear when they jump into bed;
And garters and socks, and the tiniest shoes,
And lots of nice things such as doll-babies use.

Then he makes with his tools many wonderful things,
Such as monkeys, and acrobats jumping on strings,
With many things more, for I can not tell half—
But just look at his picture, I'm sure you will laugh.

And a very wise fellow is Santa Claus, too,
He is jolly and kind, but he knows what to do;
And after his work for the day is all done,
As he sees the long rays of the bright setting sun,

He climbs to his turret, way up near the sky,
And looks o'er the world with his keen, searching eye;
Peeps into the cities, the towns, great and small,
And villages too, for he's sure to see all.

He looks into the homes of the rich and the poor,
Of those who have plenty, and those who endure;
For God's little children he finds everywhere,
The rich and the poor are alike in his care.

How funny he looks as he stands to inspect
The tree that with gifts he has lavishly decked:
He is large 'round the waist, but what care we for that—
'Tis the good-natured people who always are fat.

I told you his home was up North by the Pole,
In a palace of ice lives this happy old soul;
And the walls are as bright as the diamonds that shone
In the cave, where Aladdin went in, all alone,

To look for the lamp, which, we've often been told,
Turned iron and lead into silver and gold.
His bedstead is made of the ivory white,
And he sleeps on a mattress of down every night.

For all the day long, he is working his best,
And surely at night, the old fellow should rest.
He uses no candle, for all through the night,
The Polar-star shining, looks in with its light

Should he need for his breakfast a fish or some veal,
The sea-calves are his, and the whale, and the seal.
Where he lives there is always a cool pleasant air,
Last summer, oh! didn't we wish we were there?

He's a funny old chap, and quite shy, it would seem,
For I never but once caught a glimpse of his team;
'Twas a bright moon-lit night, and it stood in full view,
So seeing it, I can describe it to you.

When Christmas time comes, he will toil like a Turk,
For the cheery old fellow is happy at work.
With his queer-looking team, through the air he will go
And alight on the houses, all white with the snow;

And into the chimneys will dart in a trice,
When all are asleep, but the cat and the mice;
And he has to be quick, to be through in a night,
For his work must be done ere the coming of light.

Then he'll fill up the stockings with candy and toys,
And all without making a bit of a noise,
There'll be presents for Julia, and Bettie, and Jack,
And plenty more left in the old fellow's sack.

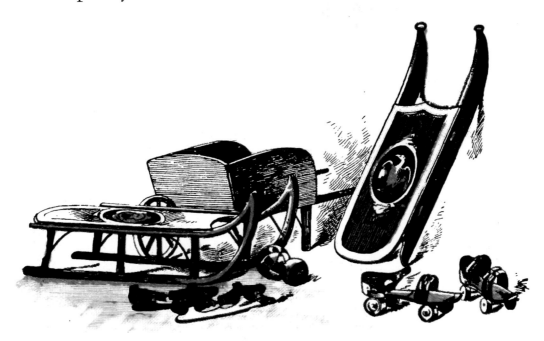

And if Evrie behaves well, and minds what is said,
Quits teasing the cat, and goes early to bed,
He'll find for his present a sled, or a gun,
A ready companion in frolic and fun.

His house in fair Santa Claus-ville, as you know,
Is near the North Pole, in the ice and the snow;
But clothed all in fur from his head to his toes,
Not a feeling of sadness the old fellow knows.

He has the most beautiful long snowy hair,
Though the top of his head is quite shiny and bare;
His dear little eyes, how they twinkle and shine,
But he never was known to drink brandy or wine.

'Tis only because he is merry and bright
That they sparkle like two little stars of the night,
And perhaps 'tis his kindness of heart showing through,
While he's planning and working dear children for you.

For good little children he's working away,
Making the toys which he'll bring them some day;
And busy all day, while he whistles and sings,
He's planning and making the funniest things.

When Christmas is over, old Santa Claus goes,
Straight home, and then takes a full week of repose,
And when all the holiday frolics are o'er,
He goes to his shop and his labors once more.

And all the long years, with his paint and his glue,
He is making new toys, little children, for you.
So be glad, and remember to do what you can,
To please and make happy this good little man.

And now, ere the story is ended, we'll give
Three cheers for old Santa Claus! Long may he live
To work for good children, and long may they try
To be good, that he never may pass any by.

Three cheers for the hero of Santa Claus-ville!
Let us echo them now, with a hearty good will.
A cleverer fellow no man ever saw,
So hail to old Santa Claus! Hip, Hip, Hurrah!

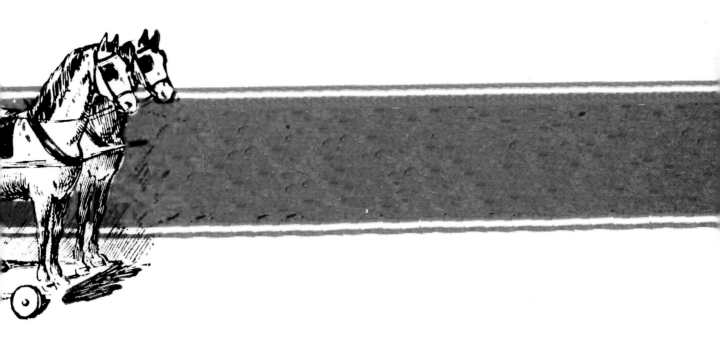

A Visit to Santa Claus

I'LL tell you a story of
Teddy Malleen
And his wonderful trip
in a flying machine.

Now Teddy was just an everyday boy,
His Mother's delight and his Father's joy.
Working and playing he spent his days,
At all sorts of things, in all sorts of ways.

And sometimes at night, when he went to bed,
Strange fancies of flying came into his head.
(While his mother patted and tucked him in)
And then his adventures would really begin.

With a chug and a whir the engine would beat,
All dressed snug and warm he would jump to his seat,
And like some great bird his ship could be seen
Sailing away with young Teddy Malleen.

'Twas a beautiful airship—strong and light—
And it sailed the fastest by pale moonlight;
Oh! Many a trip had our Teddy Malleen
In his run-about, flying machine.

On the week before Christmas when Teddy sailed forth,
He steered his ship so it went due north,
And he never faltered or stopped, because
He was going to visit old Santa Claus.

Now Santa Claus lives, as all children know,
In a land that is bounded by ice and snow,
And each snowy hummock and icy dome,
Appeared to our Teddy like Santa's home.

So he circled about like a wonderful bird
Until, far below him, he suddenly heard
A sound all good children love to hear.
'Twas the tinkling bells of eight reindeer.

Then downward he swooped—and so, in a trice
He landed with ease on a cake of ice.

And there, in a house made all of snow,
In eight box stalls which stood in a row,
Were Dasher and Dancer and Prancer and Vixen,
Comet and Cupid and Donner and Blitzen.

With Santa a little behind the scenes
Preparing their supper of Christmas greens.

The reindeer looked up in some surprise,
But Santa Claus smiled, with twinkling eyes.
Said Ted: "I've come in my airship *Pranks*
To bring you a load of Christmas thanks."

Santa Claus laughed as he said: "That's good.
But I wish you had also brought us food.

I can't make my reindeer—by any means—
Eat a single thing but Christmas greens."

Then Teddy saw Vixen, with strong white teeth
Greedily crunching a holly wreath
While Comet and Cupid (as one would know)
More daintily munched some mistletoe.

Donner and Blitzen were on their knees
Browsing on tops of hemlock trees.
While Prancer and Dasher and Dancer—three—
Devoured a municipal Christmas tree.

"You see," said Santa, "before they fly
Those many miles across the sky,
I give them as much as they can eat
To make them strong and sure and fleet."

Said Teddy, "Some boys and girls are keen
To have you come in a flying machine.
'Twould carry you quickly far and near
And save the strength of your eight reindeer."

Then the reindeer snorted and shook each horn,
And Santa Claus spoke with righteous scorn:
"Not a chick or a child but they call friend—
Would you bring their pleasure to such an end?

"I wish you could see them on Christmas Eve
When my sleigh is packed and ready to leave.
Such dancing and prancing—and then—away!
Would you spoil all their fun on Christmas Day?

"Now hurry, to work! We'll pack the toys
For all of the earth-world girls and boys,
Just carry this drum and train and track
And tuck them away inside my canvas pack.

"And then in my work shop, we'll fix the last
Of the boats that need a sail or a mast.
The dolls are dressed, and the soldiers packed,
The candy boxed, and the books all stacked.

"There's something here for every baby,
And extras, too, for new ones maybe.
It's sometimes really most bewilderin'
For every year there seem to be more children.

"And maybe you children can help me out,
(It is something I would like to talk about)
Each year my reindeers' work grows harder
While smaller each year has grown our larder.

"So tell the children, when Christmas is o'er,
To place their greens outside the door
Most gladly we'll come—with pack and sleigh,
And carry them—every one—away.

"It will give us food to last a year
Of course we keep it on ice, up here.
But now, dear Teddy, you must be gone
I see the glow of the coming dawn."

So Teddy patted each friendly deer
And said good-bye with a parting tear.
To Santa he gave a big bear hug
Then cranked his engine with turn and tug.

And he came back
     gloating and dipping
     and diving
And wasn't he lucky?
     For on his arriving
He had scarce got in
     bed when without any
     warning
In came his dear mother
     to bid him, "Good
     morning."

How Santa Filled the Christmas Stockings

THAT Christmas was coming
It was easy to see,
For Betty and Bobby
Were as meek as could be.

No more did they racket
With loud shouts through the house,
But stepped quite sedately
And as still as a mouse.

Politely they answered,
And their voices were low;
To bed they went promptly
When Mamma bade them go!

But Tommy, their brother,
Often got in a fret,
Unmindful of Christmas
And the gifts he might get.

The night before Christmas,
As they knelt by the bed:
"O please, dear old Santa,
Give us plenty!" they said.

The kiddies were chubby,
They had all curly locks,
But Betty wore stockings,
While the boys still wore socks.

So Tommy grew thoughtful
As he hung, with much care,
His socks, short and stubby,
Near his sister's long pair.

A while he lay wakeful,
As the other two slept—
He looked at the fireplace,
From his bed then he crept

For Tommy was greedy,
And he thought his socks small;
To hold all he wanted
Those would not do at all!

So Mother's long stockings
He put up in his place,
And soon was in
With a smile on his face.

Then, through the white stillness
Of the snow falling fast,
A faint tinkle sounded—
It's the reindeer, at last!

And out from the fireplace
Came a noise like a flame;
And down through the
    chimney—
It was Santa who came!

With coat red and furry,
And a pack full of toys,
All kinds of nice presents,
Both for girls and for boys.

He started to empty
All his pack near the bed,
Then he glanced at the
    stockings
And looked puzzled
    instead.

"Now, how did this
    happen?
For two boys,
    things I've here,
When surely these
    stockings
Show two girls—
    that is queer!

The good fairies blundered
When they filled up this pack,
Or marked the wrong bundle—
I've no time to go back!"

He heaped 'round the stockings
All the goodies and toys
That Betty had longed for,
But were not meant for boys.

Fine books and nice dollies,
And of games quite a score,
With work-box and ribbons,
Such a bountiful store!

A drum and a railway,
With a gay rocking horse,
And trumpet and horn, too,
Little Bob got, of course.

These partly for Tommy
Might have been, you will see
But mixed up the things got
From the lad's trickery!

And last from the fireplace
Santa drew, in delight,
A green Christmas fir-tree
Oh, so sparkling and bright!

Then up through the chimney
Santa climbed with all haste
Away to his reindeer;
Like a flash off they raced!

At daybreak, two kiddies
Found their gifts with much glee,
But Tommy, the greedy,
What a sad boy was he!

His brother and sister,
With their heads in a whirl,
Were happy, but—Tommy
Had all gifts for a girl.

When Christmas and Santa
Come next year, we may see
That Tommy, once greedy,
Will be good as can be!

Polar Bear
at the Zoo

D O you know the story of Teddy Maleen
And his wonderful trip in a flying machine?
How he made a visit,—'twas just last year—
To Santa Claus and his eight reindeer?

One lovely day when the sky
was blue,
He went with sister to visit
the zoo,
And nearly all of the time
while there
He spent at the den of the
polar bear.

For Polar Bear had such
curious ways!
All that he did was to gaze
and gaze
With a look in his eyes that
seemed to say:
"My mind and my heart
are far away

"In a land where I never
more may roam,
In my ice-bound, snow-
capped, Arctic
home."

That night when Teddy was snug in bed,
Visions of Polar Bear filled his head.
Thought Teddy: "Oh, wouldn't it be just grand
To carry him back to his native land?"

Then just as he closed his sleepy eyes,
He heard out of doors in the starry skies,
The gentle hum of his airship *Pranks*
And Teddy murmured a
    word of thanks,
As, donning his coat
    and a cap of seal,
He jumped to his seat
    at the steering wheel.

Then out and away in
    the friendly night
He sailed and
    sailed by the pale
    moonlight,
When lo! in only a
    minute or two
He found himself
    once more at
    the zoo.

He muffled his engine with greatest care
And landed quite close to the polar bear.
Then tiptoeing lightly took a peep
At the kindly keeper fast asleep.

With softest of voices he whispered low—
"Dear Polar Bear, would you like to go
On a midnight journey through the air?
Do say that you will, dear Polar Bear!"

The bear arose and with lumbering feet
Climbed aboard and was strapped to his seat.
Then softly the engine started its purring,
As upward the airship went merrily whirring.

They were warm, of course, in their coats of fur,
And to neither of them did it occur
That Teddy boy's coat, though fit for a king,
Was not like Polar Bear's fur—"the real thing."

Said Teddy, "Dear bear, does the blue book give
The route to the place where you used to live?"
"As to that," said the bear, "it was at the Pole
Next door to the Arctic swimming hole.

"I'll take the glasses, and when I spy
The northern lights in the polar sky,
And when I behold an ice-capped dome,
I'll know we must be nearing home."

He had scarce stopped speaking, when in the north
The shifting lights came straggling forth;
Now pale, now bright, now low, now high,
Like rainbow ribbons in the sky.

"Aha!" said the bear, "there stands the Pole,
And right beyond it the swimming hole!"
So down swooped Ted from his wondrous
    heights,
Right over and through the northern lights.

With ease he circled
    around the Pole,
And dipping close to the
    swimming hole,
He landed his ship with never a
    shock,
At just midnight by the
    polar clock.

The bears came running from near and far
To see what looked like a shooting star.
But coming closer, their wonder grew
At sight of Polar Bear from the zoo.

They had heard by wireless of Teddy Maleen
And his trip to Santa by flying machine,
So they recognized him, of course, at once,
And welcomed them both with loving grunts.
Around the Pole they capered with vim;
Then all went in for an ice cold swim.

But Oh! how quickly the time did fly!
The northern lights grew dim in the sky,
And Teddy was wondering what he could do
To coax Mr. Polar Bear back to the zoo.

When suddenly, greatly to his surprise,
The bear looked up with his dreamy eyes,
And said: "Well Teddy, alas, alack!
I think we'd better be getting back.

"To tell you the truth I musn't stay,
Because tomorrow is Saturday.
I have an appointment with two small girls
With big brown eyes, and sun-kissed curls.

"And then there's Jimmie, the boy who's lame—
I couldn't be happy, if he came
And looked for me, as he's sure to do,
And found I'd run away from the zoo.

"There's a little old lady, who every day
Just smiles at me in her friendly way.
Then there's my keeper so kind and true,
Oh no, dear Teddy, it never would do!

"I've enjoyed my visit to the Pole;
I've liked my bath in the swimming hole;
But not for worlds would I stay away
From my dear little friends on Saturday."

They jumped in the ship and soon were far
Out in the sky like a twinkling star.
They floated home by the milky way,
And landed safely at break of day.

Said Teddy at breakfast,—"I'm very glad
My polar bear friend isn't really sad.
When he looks at you with mournful eyes
It's only his way of looking wise!

"And there's nothing on earth he'd rather do
Than just be Polar Bear at the zoo!"

ALSO AVAILABLE